Disney
Animals
Storybook Collection

Disney PRESS

LOS ANGELES • NEW YORK

Contents

"Pua and Heihei" written by Suzanne Francis and illustrated by Denise Shimabukuro and the Disney Storybook Art Team. Copyright © 2016 Disney Enterprises, Inc.

"The Surprise Party" written by Victoria Saxon and illustrated by the Disney Storybook Art Team. Copyright © 2019 Disney Enterprises, Inc.

"Briar Rose to the Rescue" written by Tracey West, illustrated by Alvin S. White Studio, and originally published in the book *Disney's Year Book 2003* by Scholastic Inc. Copyright © 2003 Disney Enterprises, Inc.

"Figaro's Day Out" written by Brooke Vitale and illustrated by the Disney Storybook Art Team. Copyright © 2019 Disney Enterprises, Inc.

"The Story of Dante" written by Roni Capin Rivera-Ashford and Daniel Rivera Ashford and illustrated by the Disney Storybook Art Team. Copyright © 2018 Disney Enterprises, Inc., and Pixar.

"Thunderbolt Patch" written by Melissa Lagonegro and illustrated by the Disney Storybook Art Team. Copyright © 2014 Disney Enterprises, Inc.

"The Great Cub-House Search" written by Victoria Saxon and illustrated by the Disney Storybook Art Team. Copyright © 2019 Disney Enterprises, Inc.

"Hustle Up" written by Suzanne Francis and illustrated by the Disney Storybook Art Team. Copyright © 2016 Disney Enterprises, Inc.

"A New Reindeer Friend" written by Jessica Julius and illustrated by the Disney Storybook Art Team. Copyright © 2014 Disney Enterprises, Inc.

"A Delicious Duo" written by Lauren Clauss and illustrated by the Disney Storybook Art Team. Copyright © 2018 Disney Enterprises, Inc., and Pixar.

"It Takes Two" written by Victoria Saxon and illustrated by the Disney Storybook Art Team. Copyright © 2019 Disney Enterprises, Inc.

"Donald Duck and the Dairy Farm" illustrated by the Disney Storybook Art Team and adapted from the book *Let's Go to the Dairy Farm,* written by Barbara Bazaldua, illustrated by DiCicco Digital Arts, and originally published by Random House. Copyright © 2015 Disney Enterprises, Inc.

"Who Cares? Pooh Cares!" written by Bonnie Worth and illustrated by Samantha Hollister. Copyright © 2007 Disney Enterprises, Inc. Based on the "Winnie the Pooh" works by A. A. Milne and E. H. Shepard.

"Timothy's Big Day" written by Brooke Vitale and illustrated by the Disney Storybook Art Team. Copyright © 2019 Disney Enterprises, Inc.

"Who Needs a Hug?" written by Beth Sycamore and illustrated by the Disney Storybook Art Team. Copyright © 2017 Disney Enterprises, Inc., and Pixar.

"Barking Up the Right Tree" written by Lara Bergen and illustrated by the Disney Storybook Art Team. Copyright © 2018 Disney Enterprises, Inc.

"Bath Time for Lucifer" written by Rachael Upton and illustrated by the Disney Storybook Art Team. Copyright © 2019 Disney Enterprises, Inc.

"Thumper Finds a Friend" written by Laura Driscoll and illustrated by Lori Tyminski, Maria Elena Naggi, Giorgio Vallorani, and Doug Ball. Copyright © 2009 Disney Enterprises, Inc.

Published by Disney Press, an imprint of Disney Book Group. No part of this book may be reproduced or transmitted in any form or by any means, electronic or mechanical, including photocopying, recording, or by any information storage and retrieval system, without written permission from the publisher.

For information address Disney Press, 1200 Grand Central Avenue, Glendale, California 91201.

Printed in the United States of America

First Hardcover Edition, September 2019

Library of Congress Control Number: 2018967198

10 9 8 7 6 5 4 3 2 1

ISBN 978-1-368-04198-0

FAC-038091-19221

For more Disney Press fun, visit www.disneybooks.com

PUA AND HEIHEI

THE FEAST TO WELCOME spring was about to start. Moana and Gramma Tala were busy collecting shells. Moana's pet pig, Pua, tried to help, but the shells he found were never empty.

Moana bent down and picked up a small pink one. "What do you think?" she asked.

Gramma Tala inspected it. "Yes! That looks right for a chief."

Moana was making her father a surprise gift for the feast: an anklet.

Moana strung the shell onto the anklet
and held it up proudly. "Done," she said. "Now
I can give it to him right at the start of the feast." Just then,
Heihei, the foolish village rooster, ran by them wearing part of a coconut
on his head. "Silly Heihei," Moana said, removing the coconut.

In the village, preparations for the feast had begun. While everyone was hard at work, Heihei just got in the way.

Men were busy building the *umu*, an underground oven. They piled up pieces of wood and the dried husks and shells of coconuts. After they started the fire, they added rocks.

Heihei kept getting closer and closer to the hot rocks.

"You'll set yourself on fire, you silly bird!" one of the men yelled, chasing him away.

Heihei ran away and stepped on a partially finished platter woven from pandan leaves. His tiny foot got trapped. But he didn't even notice as he dragged the large platter behind him.

Gramma Tala attempted to catch him, but Heihei avoided her, leaving a mess in his wake.

Moana and Gramma Tala stopped when they saw Chief Tui approaching. Gramma Tala immediately stepped on Heihei's platter to hold it, and the rooster, in place.

Moana quickly hid the anklet inside her belt, hoping her father wouldn't notice.

"I just wanted to see how everything was going," Chief Tui said.

Meanwhile, Heihei was pecking and pulling at Gramma Tala's skirt.

As soon as Chief Tui left,

Gramma Tala reached for Heihei, but

she slipped on the platter! Fortunately,

Moana was there to catch her.

Nobody noticed when the anklet dropped from Moana's belt. It landed

around Heihei's neck, and he dashed away.

"That is it!" Gramma Tala said, grabbing a handwoven leaf basket.

Heihei didn't see her coming. He was too busy pecking at a rock.

In one fell swoop, Gramma Tala trapped Heihei underneath the basket . . . and then cinched it shut! But Gramma Tala had been so focused on catching the rooster that she hadn't noticed the anklet around his neck.

"You can't keep him in there forever, Gramma," said Moana.

"But we can keep him in there for a little while," said Gramma Tala. "At least until we're done with the feast."

Moana agreed it was a good idea . . . so Gramma Tala put the basket aside.

Then Moana checked her belt. She gasped when she realized the anklet was missing. "Oh, no!"

"Perhaps we should retrace our steps," said Gramma Tala.

Just then, Pua spotted the basket. He saw Heihei's beak sticking out between the gaps in the woven leaves. When he looked closer, Pua noticed the anklet around the rooster's neck. He was determined to retrieve it for Moana.

But first Pua had to open the basket. He rolled it over and over, but that didn't work. The basket was just too strong.

Then he tossed a coconut high into the air toward the basket. But all that did was knock the basket over.

Next Pua put the basket on top of a stick. Then he backed up and took a running start. Pua jumped onto the stick, and the basket went flying through the air!

Plop! It fell to the ground. But the basket was still tightly shut.

Pua had to think of another idea, and fast. He had to get the anklet to Moana in time for the feast.

On the ground, he saw a long vine. He picked it up, and trotted back to the basket. Pua looped the vine around the basket and dragged it along, running as fast as he could. Heihei's legs slipped out and he ran to keep up.

When Pua heard music, he knew the feast was about to begin. He had to do something drastic.

He dragged the basket toward a slender tree and tossed it onto a branch. Then he jumped up after it.

When Pua bounced on the branch, Heihei's basket flew into the air and then back down to the branch again. The higher Pua bounced, the higher the basket flew.

Finally, Pua bounced so high that the branch flung the basket straight into him! The two animals soared through the air.

Pua and Heihei squealed and clucked.

When they hit the ground, the basket finally opened! Pua was thrilled. He could get the anklet to Moana!

But the force of the fall caused them to roll . . . and roll . . . and roll, right into a large fishing net.

16

Though the feast had started, Pua and Heihei rolled right up to Moana!
Moana untangled them and gasped when she saw the anklet around
Pua's snout. "You found it!" she said, giving him a big hug.

Later that evening, Moana gave Chief Tui the anklet, and he proudly put it on.

"I love it," he said.

As Moana and her father hugged, Pua heard a strange sound. It was Heihei. The rooster couldn't cluck because his beak was buried in a piece of driftwood. He'd also gotten tangled up in pieces of the basket again.

Fortunately, Pua had become an expert at getting Heihei out of tricky situations.

The Surprise Party

Early one morning, Thomas O'Malley yawned, stretched, and found three little kittens jumping on his bed. Marie, Berlioz, and Toulouse began to sing cheerily while Duchess presented O'Malley with a dish of cream!

"Happy birthday!" the cats sang out. "Happy birthday to you, dear Abraham DeLacey Giuseppe Casey Thomas O'Malley!"

"Now, children," Duchess began. "Who wants to give Thomas his birthday present first?"

"I do, I do!" Toulouse replied. "Follow me, Mr. O'Malley!"

"Yeah," said Berlioz. "Follow him!"

As soon as O'Malley's back was turned, Duchess whispered to Berlioz and Marie: "Come, children! Let's get on with our plans for Thomas's surprise party!"

Toulouse led O'Malley into the sunroom.

"This is where I do my greatest work," Toulouse announced. "And today I'm gonna paint your portrait. Face this way, please, and don't move!"

Squish! Splurt! Splat! Toulouse began squirting paint from various tubes.

O'Malley was so busy watching Toulouse that he didn't see what was happening behind him.

A little while later, Toulouse finished his painting and presented it proudly to O'Malley.

"That's real swell, Toulouse," O'Malley said. "I don't suppose you could teach me how to do that."

"Sure!" Toulouse replied. "I can teach ya!" He smothered a smile. The birthday surprise plans were right on track!

Toulouse showed O'Malley how to mix paints to get different colors.

Then they outlined a picture. Finally, they painted . . . and painted . . . and painted!

"I never had such birthday fun in my life!" O'Malley said when they were finished. "I can't wait to show this to Scat Cat and the band when we jam!"

Just then, Marie and Berlioz walked into the room.

"Our turn, our turn!" Marie said to O'Malley, climbing to her spot atop the piano. "Would you like to hear some scales and arpeggios?"

"We planned a special birthday song just for you!" Berlioz said.

"Wanna hear it?"

"Well, sure I do!" O'Malley said.

Berlioz cracked his toes while Marie moved to the other side of the piano and sat up straight. She made sure O'Malley was looking at her—not outside, where the others were setting up his surprise party.

"Okay," Berlioz said at last. "Are you ready?"

"Ready!" O'Malley replied.

Berlioz stretched along the keyboard and played their new song while

Marie sang. O'Malley was loving the tempo and couldn't believe they had

written him his very own tune.

"You can join us if you want to, Mr. O'Malley," Marie urged.

Soon O'Malley was singing along. "Thank you for the best birthday song

I've ever heard!"

As early evening approached, Duchess intercepted O'Malley.

"Do you want to go for a birthday stroll?" she asked.

"Well, sure," O'Malley said. "That old band can wait. There's nothing I'd rather do than go on a birthday walk—er, stroll—with you."

When they reached the end of the garden, Duchess pulled a wrapped gift from behind a rosebush.

"Happy birthday, dear Thomas," she said, presenting it to him.

"A bow tie! Thanks, Duchess," he said. "Between you and those kittens, this has been a terrific birthday!"

"It's not over yet, you know," Duchess told him. "We do have one last surprise for you."

Duchess led O'Malley into the dining room.

"I hope everything is to your liking," Madame said to O'Malley.

Toulouse, Berlioz, and Marie were there with Roquefort, too.

"Happy birthday!" they all called out.

They had prepared all his favorite foods. O'Malley and Duchess even shared a salmon soufflé.

"Say, what a terrific birthday!" O'Malley said. "I do think it's almost time for bed, though, little ones."

"Before we go to bed, can we go look at the stars?" Marie asked.

"Oh, yes," Duchess agreed as they all headed outside. "That's a wonderful idea. And Thomas! I have to confess—the dinner was your second-to-last birthday surprise. . . ."

"Surprise!" yelled Duchess and the kittens.

"Surprise!" hollered Scat Cat and the band.

"Wow!" O'Malley exclaimed. Turning to Duchess and the kittens, he asked, "How did you pull this off? You were with me all day!"

Marie giggled. "Well, sometimes some of us were with you—"

"While others of us were preparing," Duchess concluded.

When the night finally ended, O'Malley turned to Duchess and the kittens. "Thanks for the best birthday I ever had! It's over now, right?" he said, laughing.

"Yes," Toulouse whispered sleepily. "Happy birthday to you, Abraham DeLacey Giuseppe Casey Thomas O'Malley!"

Briar Rose to the Rescue

"Oh, drat," *Flora said.* "We're out of wood!"

"No wood?" Merryweather asked. "But how will we stay warm overnight? Why, with no fire, we'll freeze!"

Briar Rose smiled at her aunt. She loved her dearly, but Merryweather certainly had a flair for the dramatic.

"I'll go fetch some more," Briar Rose offered. Then, putting on her cloak, she stepped out of the cottage. "I'll be right back!" she called.

Briar Rose didn't have to go far to find wood. By the time she had taken a few steps into the forest, her arms were full. But as she turned to go home, Briar Rose heard a noise.

"Hoo! Hoo!"

Briar Rose spun around to see her friend the owl perched on a tree branch.

"Why, hello there," Briar Rose called back. "How are you this evening?"

"Hoo! Hoo!" the owl called again. He flapped his wings frantically and hopped up and down on the branch. Then, with one more hoot, he flew deeper into the forest.

Briar Rose frowned. Her animal friends were usually quite calm. It was not like the owl to seem so upset. She hoped nothing was wrong.

Setting down the pile of wood she had collected, she followed him.

The owl landed on a large oak tree. Briar Rose knew that a family of rabbits lived inside. Her heart pounded. "Is something wrong with the bunnies?" she asked.

Briar Rose knelt down and looked into the hollow tree trunk. The mother rabbit was there, anxiously fussing over her babies.

"One . . . two . . ." Briar Rose counted. "Where is the third bunny? There should be one more!"

Now Briar Rose knew why the owl had seemed so upset. A baby bunny was missing!

"Don't worry. I'll find him," Briar Rose promised. "And you'll help me, won't you, Owl?"

"Hoo! Hoo!" the owl agreed.

Briar Rose stood up and looked at the forest trail. The sky was growing dark, but she could just make out tiny paw prints on the ground.

"Look!" she said, pointing at the trail. "He went that way. Let's go!"

Briar Rose followed the trail, with the owl flying close behind. But the deeper she got into the woods, the more the trees blocked the moonlight. "Soon I won't be able to see a thing!" she said.

As she spoke, a cloud of fireflies flew up to her. They blinked on and off, lighting up the path. Briar Rose smiled, surprised. "Oh! Thank you!" she said. "That's *much* better."

The paw prints led to a stream and then disappeared.

"Hmmm," Briar Rose said. "The little guy must have hopped across the stream on those rocks."

Briar Rose started to step on the nearest rock. But it wasn't a rock. It was a turtle shell! A sleepy turtle poked her head out of the water.

"Oh, my!" Briar Rose said, pulling her foot back. "I'm so sorry. I didn't mean to step on you. I was just trying to get across the stream. Your shell looked like a stone. Are there any more of you in the water?"

At the commotion, four more sleepy turtles popped their heads up and looked around.

"I'm sorry to wake you," Briar Rose said, "but I don't want to step on you by mistake!" Briar Rose bent down and peered at the turtles' shells. Now that she knew what she was looking for, she could see the difference between the turtles and the rocks.

"Thank you," she said as she carefully stepped across the rocks. "You can go back to sleep now."

On the other side of the stream, Briar Rose spotted the bunny's paw prints. All around her, the sounds of the forest filled the air. Crickets chirped. Tiny wood mice scurried through the pine needles. Bats flapped their wings as they swept through the trees. But Briar Rose barely noticed. She was too focused on finding the bunny.

Suddenly, two yellow eyes appeared in some nearby bushes. Frightened, the fireflies fled. The owl let out a startled hoot. But Briar Rose walked toward them.

"Who's there?" she asked.

A small red fox trotted out of the bushes.

Briar Rose smiled. "Hello there!" she said. Briar Rose pointed to the trail of footprints. It had grown so dark that she could barely see them. "I'm looking for a lost bunny. Have you seen him?"

The fox looked at Briar Rose, confused. Then she began to sniff the ground. A moment later, she turned and walked away.

Briar Rose quickly set off after the fox.

"Hoo! Hoo!" Suddenly, the owl let out a warning cry and flew in front of Briar Rose. She stopped and looked down—right at the edge of a cliff! The fox was making her way across a fallen tree to get to the other side. But Briar Rose had nearly stepped over the edge!

"Thank you, Owl," Briar Rose said. "It's a good thing that you can see so well at night!"

Then, following the fox's lead, she carefully walked across the fallen tree.

The fox led Briar Rose to the edge of the forest. Ahead she could see a cottage with a big vegetable garden.

"Thank you," Briar Rose called out to her new friend. But the fox had already disappeared into the woods.

Stepping out of the forest, Briar Rose headed toward the cottage. The moon shone brightly overhead, and she could easily see the missing bunny sleeping happily in a patch of lettuce.

Laughing softly, Briar Rose picked up the bunny and made her way back over the fallen tree, across the stream, and to the hollow tree that was home to the family of rabbits.

"Here you are," Briar Rose said, placing the bunny inside the hollow. "Safe and sound."

The bunny's mother, brother, and sister were so happy the little bunny was home. They all snuggled up, ready for bedtime.

Briar Rose smiled at the rabbits. Then she yawned. "Oh, my, I'm getting sleepy, too! I need to get back to the cottage."

Gathering her firewood, Briar Rose returned to the cottage, where the three anxious aunts were waiting for her.

"Where were you?" Flora asked.

"We were so worried about you!" Fauna exclaimed.

"We went to look for you, but all we could find was an abandoned pile of wood," Merryweather said. "We thought someone had kidnapped you!"

"I'm sorry," Briar Rose said. "It was an emergency. Besides, who would want to hurt *me*?"

"Now, now, Merryweather, she's just fine," Fauna said. Then, turning to Briar Rose, she added, "How about some cake and a nice hot cup of tea, and you can tell us everything that happened?"

So Briar Rose and her aunts settled in for the night, and the girl told them all about her adventure.

Disney
Pinocchio

FIGARO'S DAY OUT

FIGARO SCOWLED AT PINOCCHIO from the corner. Ever since the Blue Fairy had brought the puppet to life, things had changed.

Before, Figaro had slept in Geppetto's bed. He had eaten all his meals beside the wood-carver, and he had been the one Geppetto told his stories to. But now it seemed like Geppetto only had time for Pinocchio.

Suddenly, a dragonfly flew past Figaro's nose. The kitten chased the bug through the cottage and out the front door. But before he could get his paw on it, the dragonfly flew out of reach.

Just then, Figaro heard a voice. "Here, kitty, kitty. Here, kitty, kitty."

Figaro happily trotted across the street to where a little girl stood with her mother. If Geppetto didn't have time for him, he'd get his snuggles somewhere else.

"Oh, aren't you just the sweetest little kitty," the girl said. "I'm Victoria. I wish I could keep playing with you, but it's time for me to go home."

Giving Figaro one last rub between the eyes, the girl stood up, and she and her mother walked away.

Keeping his eyes on the girl, Figaro followed behind, weaving down street after street.

Finally, Victoria and her mother reached a small building. Figaro tried to follow them inside, but the girl's mother stopped him.

"Oh, please, Mama," Victoria pleaded. "I'll take good care of him."

"You know my rule," she said. "No animals."

"I'm sorry, kitty," Victoria said. "I'm not allowed to have pets. You go on home now."

Figaro looked around. He had been so focused on following the girl that he hadn't paid attention to where he was walking. He realized he had no idea where he was. Nothing looked familiar. How was he going to find his way home if he didn't know where he was?

Figaro began to walk, but soon it started to rain.

Figaro thought about the last time he'd been so wet. He had been outside playing while Pinocchio and Geppetto did their shopping, when suddenly it had started to rain. By the time the two got home, the poor kitten was shivering. Pinocchio had carried him inside and dried him off with a warm blanket.

Suddenly, the little kitten's stomach began to grumble. It must be dinnertime.

A little way down the road, Figaro spotted a market.

Looking up at a fish seller, he meowed loudly. But the man just swatted him away.

"Off you go," he said, brushing Figaro aside with a broom. "Find your food somewhere else."

Figaro's stomach growled again. It seemed that he might be going to sleep hungry.

At the thought of sleep, Figaro yawned. Perhaps it would be best to find a

place to spend the night. But everywhere Figaro tried to rest was already taken.

He was chased out of a dark alley by an angry cat.

In the park, a pack of vicious dogs snarled
and barked at him until he ran away.

And under the
bridge, he was
hurried off by a
family of ducks!

Spotting an empty step in front of a shop, Figaro lay down and put his head on his paws. The little kitten began to whimper. He had never been so cold, so hungry, so tired, or so lonely in his whole life.

As he tried to get comfortable, Figaro thought of Pinocchio. Pinocchio had set up a nice spot near the fireplace for Figaro and even saved his allowance for a cozy blanket. Figaro started to feel bad for being angry with Pinocchio.

The next morning, Figaro awoke
to the sound of someone calling his
name.

"There you are!"
Pinocchio cried. "Father
and I have been looking
for you all night."

Suddenly, Pinocchio
noticed that the little
kitten was shivering.
"Oh, you're freezing,"
he said. "Come
along. We'd
best get
you home
at once!"

Back at the wood-carver's workshop, Geppetto built up the fire and settled Figaro in his warm bed beside the fireplace. Pinocchio gave the kitten a big bowl of cream and a plate of fish.

"There now," Pinocchio said. "You should be feeling better in no time."

Geppetto smiled at his son. "You take such good care of Figaro, there's nothing left for me to do for him. You certainly love him, don't you?"

Pinocchio sat down beside the kitten and began to pet him. "Oh, Figaro," he said. "What would we have done if we lost you? We do love you so."

Figaro looked up at the boy, surprised. That was the first time Pinocchio had ever said he loved Figaro. But as Figaro thought of all the nice things Pinocchio had done for him, he realized the boy had been showing the kitten his love all along.

Nuzzling Pinocchio, Figaro snuggled up on the boy's lap. Warm, dry, and with his belly full of food, the kitten began to drift off to sleep.

Perhaps, he thought, Pinocchio wasn't so bad after all. In fact, having another person love him sounded just fine to Figaro. And he realized he was starting to love the boy, too.

The Story of Dante

Miles away from the nearest town sat an abandoned farm. Living there was hard, but one scrappy puppy made the best of it. He was a Xoloitzcuintli (show-loh-eets-KWEENT-lee), or Xolo (show-loh) for short.

Every morning, he stretched and yawned, snacked on vegetables from a once-loved garden, and quenched his thirst with rainwater from a nearby trough.

The puppy didn't always know what to do, but he learned how to follow his instincts.

After a time, he knew he had to move on from the farm. There wasn't much left for him to eat, and he wanted to find friends.

So he began his journey.

He walked for a while and arrived in the cemetery of a town called Santa Cecilia. The day before was Día de los Muertos, and the townspeople had left quite a scene behind.

The Xolo's nose led him to hidden treats and treasures. There were so many things to see and eat that the eager puppy didn't know what to try first.

Once the puppy had filled his belly with delicious food, he settled under the boughs of an oak tree. He was ready for a siesta.

After his nap, he saw that many other stray animals had arrived in the cemetery.

Dogs, cats, and birds romped, played, and flitted around the tombstones. Then the Xolo joined the fun! He realized he had found amigos.

Just then, the pup's nose caught a whiff of something amazing! He loved playtime, but his curiosity had been piqued. He followed the delicious aroma to see where it might lead.

His nose led him into town. But nothing could have prepared him for what he saw next. Santa Cecilia's main street was filled with exquisite food and delicacies. It was glorious.

The Xolo spotted a little boy who seemed to know everyone. So the pup followed him in search of a decent meal.

It wasn't long before the boy—his name was Miguel—noticed the puppy and started introducing him to the nice people in town: Don Pancho the baker, Luisita the street taco vendor, Señor González the butcher, and Señora Sena the teacher.

Thanks to them, the puppy tried all sorts of delicious treats.

Fortunately, they always enjoyed the puppy's visits, too, and would make sure he never went hungry again.

But there were also people who felt the Xolo was a nuisance.

There was Chato the garbage collector, who always yelled at the street dog to get off his truck.

And Señor Lucas—never again would the puppy trespass on *his* property. Once, the Xolo crawled underneath his barbed wire fence and narrowly avoided getting a painful scratch on his back.

Then there was Abuelita. She made the most incredible tamales!

The puppy thought he could sneak one without getting caught.

"Get out of here!" she'd yell as the pup fled the hacienda.

He often heard her grumble, "Street dogs . . .

the only thing I like less

than musicians."

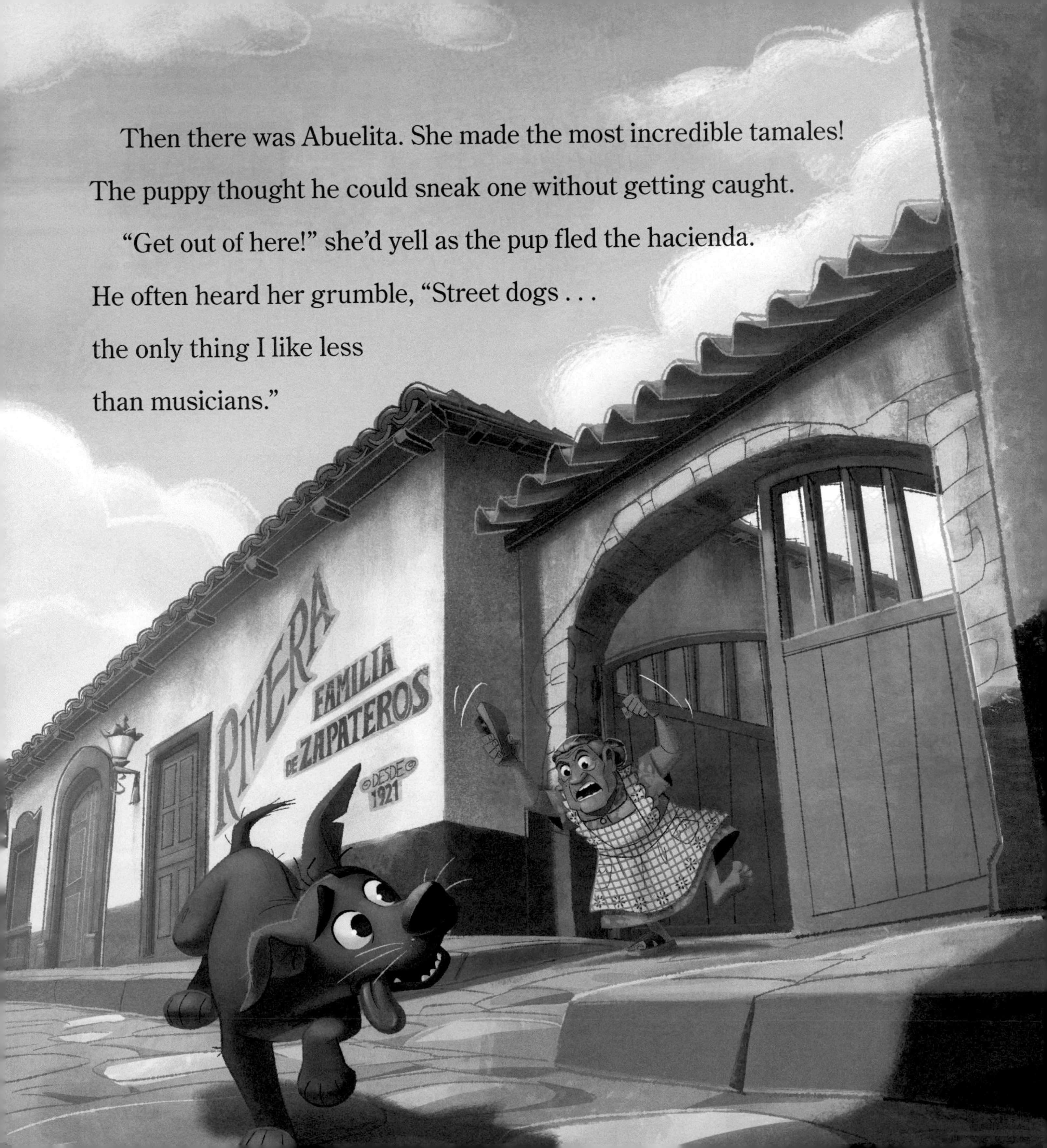

After months of learning how to survive in Santa Cecilia, the puppy got

bigger and stronger . . . and so did his friendship with Miguel. The two

would spend their days having fun and being goofy.

The dog often joined Miguel as he shined shoes in the plaza. They would always listen to the mariachis. This became one of the dog's favorite routines. The weather, music, and company made for a perfect afternoon.

However, these happy occasions did not always go according to plan. If Abuelita saw Miguel with the Xolo, her sandal would go flying! The dog would run away to keep from getting hit.

The Xolo knew he shouldn't follow Miguel home after times like those. So he'd sneak back to his haven in the cemetery and look forward to his next encounter with Miguel.

One morning, the Xolo awoke to the beautiful sounds of a guitar. He followed la música, hoping it would lead him to his amigo . . . and found Miguel in the shade of a tree. The dog stayed with Miguel while he practiced his music.

A few days had passed since the visit under the tree, and the Xolo missed his friend! He realized that Miguel was the best part of Santa Cecilia. He'd risk just about anything to be near him.

The dog usually followed his nose, but this time . . .

. . . he followed his heart. And what he found was a warm embrace.

"What are you doing here?" Miguel laughed as the Xolo licked his face. "I know you're not my dog. . . . You belong to all of Santa Cecilia. But everyone needs a name. I'm going to call you . . . Dante. Okay?"

Dante thought his new name was perfect.

Thunderbolt Patch

Every evening, Pongo, Perdita, and their fifteen Dalmatian puppies gathered around the television to watch the heroic adventures of Thunderbolt the dog. The puppies would stare wide-eyed as Thunderbolt saved the day from all sorts of thieves and villains.

Patch wanted to be just like Thunderbolt!

After the show ended, it would be time for the puppies to go to sleep so
Pongo and Perdita could go on a walk with their humans.

"Come along, children," said Pongo one evening.

"I'm hungry, Mother," whined Rolly the pudgy pup.

"Can't we stay up a bit longer?" pleaded Patch.

"It's time for sleep now, my dears," Perdita replied.

All the puppies settled into bed—except for Patch.

Patch didn't want to go to sleep. He wanted to go on an adventure, like Thunderbolt. He wanted to save the day from all sorts of thieves and villains.

And when the puppy heard a strange scurrying sound nearby, Patch knew he had his chance.

"Look!" whispered Patch, pointing at a mouse. "It's a big bad bandit! We've got to catch him!"

The puppies scampered out of bed and snuck upstairs after the fearsome outlaw.

"Follow me," whispered Patch, pretending to be Thunderbolt. "That nasty scoundrel is heading toward the music room."

"Where could he be hiding?" Pepper wondered.

"Let me know if you find any food," said Rolly as he nosed a nearby wastebasket.

"There!" Lucky yelped. "Behind the bin! He's heading for the door!"

Before the puppies could catch the bandit, they heard someone coming up the stairs. It was Nanny! If she caught the pups out of bed, they would be in big trouble.

"Hide," whispered Patch.

Each pup hid in the perfect spot, hoping Nanny wouldn't suspect they were on a nighttime adventure.

"Now what's all this noise?" asked Nanny, looking about the music room.

As the pups held their breath, Patch spied the scoundrel slipping back downstairs. Fortunately, Nanny didn't spot a single Dalmatian pup . . . or the bandit!

When the coast was clear, the puppies resumed their chase throughout the house. They traveled down the steps . . . into the living room . . . and eventually outside.

"The thief is escaping!" shouted Patch. "After him!"

"Catching culprits makes me hungry,"
Rolly whined.

Fortunately, the back door was ajar, and the pups could easily slip out and continue the chase.

"He's headed toward the courtyard," said Patch. "We can't lose him, men!"

While the puppies searched for the scoundrel, Rolly decided to search for a snack.

He found a berry bush. But when one of the berries slipped under the gate, the chubby pup spotted something foul.

"Cruella De Vil!" he gasped. "She's coming this way!"

"Quietly now," whispered Thunderbolt Patch as he and the puppies followed the bandit back into the house.

"That sly burglar must be in here somewhere," said Patch as they

searched the entire kitchen.

"There he is!" shouted Rolly when he spotted the mouse getting away.

"And he has cheese—yum!" Rolly darted toward the bandit.

But they both suddenly disappeared in a cloud of white!

"That pup doesn't have any spots," said Patch, looking at Rolly. "He must

be the *real* intruder!"

The puppies all pounced on Rolly, but soon Penny spotted Pongo and Perdita outside.

"Mother and Father are coming!" she shouted. "Everyone back to bed!"

"Come along, chaps!" shouted the leader of the pack. "Thunderbolt Patch will save the day!"

When Pongo and Perdita returned from their walk, they peeked in on their precious puppies and found them curled up in bed—just as they had left them.

The Great
Cub-House Search

"**S**imba!" **Sarabi called out** to her son. "Where are you? It's time for your bath."

"Mo-om, I'm not even dirty!" Simba called back before quietly sighing.

It was always time for something—and that something was always something he didn't want to do.

Today is going to be different, Simba thought. *Today is a day for adventure.*

"Hey, Nala," Simba said. "I have an idea. I'm gonna find a clubhouse, and we can hang out there and do whatever we want! Do you wanna go with me?"

"You mean a cub-house?" Nala chuckled. "That sounds great!"

"Simba," Sarabi said, having overheard them. "You can go, but you must be home before dark. And wait for Zazu!"

"Sure, Mom!" Simba shouted. Turning to Nala, he added, "If Zazu can catch us! Come on! Follow me!"

Simba was taking Nala to a hiding place that might be perfect for their cub-house. He couldn't wait to see what she thought of it!

"Isn't this the best hideout?" Simba said as he leaped up on a large rock. "We can do whatever we want, make it our own, and Zazu will never look for us here."

Just then, Scar walked around the corner.

"Ah, my favorite nephew," Scar grumbled.

"Uncle Scar, I'm your *only* nephew," Simba said, laughing. "Look! I brought my friend Nala!"

Scar did not seem pleased. "What are you two doing here?" he asked.

"We're looking for our very own cub-house," Simba explained. "Come on, Nala! I'll show you the dark part of the cave."

Scar scowled. He didn't want his nephew hanging around his home.

"Well, if you must," Scar began, already plotting how to get rid of Simba. "But did I mention that Zazu is coming for a visit soon? He checks up on me, you know. . . ."

"We were kinda trying to avoid Zazu," Simba said.

"Time to go check out another cub-house option, I guess!" Nala told Simba.

"I think you're right! Bye, Uncle Scar!" Simba called.

The pair ran off before Zazu could catch up to them.

"Where should we go now?" Nala asked.

Simba thought for a moment. He looked back at Pride Rock.

It wasn't too far away.

"I know!" he said at last. "We can go near the watering hole!

There are always lots of animals there."

Lost in the crowd, the two friends could do whatever they wanted!

"Check it out!" Nala exclaimed, and she jumped and splashed in the water.

"Hey, you got me wet!" Simba yelled.

But it was so much fun that he soon jumped in, too! The two cubs ran and played together. This spot seemed perfect for their cub-house.

The fun and games continued . . . until Simba bumped right into an elephant's leg!

"Whoa! Watch out!" Nala said.

They were soon surrounded by a parade of elephants, none of whom seemed to notice the two lion cubs running among them.

"Nala, look out!" Simba cried. A crash of rhinoceroses was rushing straight toward his friend. He raced over and pushed her out of the way just in time . . .

but ran right into a colony of flamingos!

"Sorry!" he hollered as he scrambled away.

"I think I'm ready to leave now," Nala said as she caught her breath.

"Me too," Simba agreed. "I'm not sure this is the place for our cub-house."

The tired cubs started out across the savanna, but then Simba got an idea.

"Follow me!" he said to Nala.

Simba led Nala straight to the base of Rafiki's tree.

"Now this is what I call a perfect cub-house," Simba said as he began to climb up into the tree.

"Nice," Nala replied as she followed him. "I'm gonna find my own branch."

The two friends were so exhausted from their adventures that they settled down to nap for a while.

"What are you doing?" Rafiki asked, waking the two cubs abruptly.

Simba looked up groggily. "Wha—?"

"You don't belong here!" Rafiki said. He scratched his chin and muttered, "You belong up there!"

He pointed toward Pride Rock.

The cubs looked toward their home. They could see everyone gathering for supper, and they spotted their mothers looking for them.

"We were supposed to be home before dark," Nala said, "and I am kinda getting hungry."

"Me too," Simba added.

The cubs thanked Rafiki and then headed back to Pride Rock.

"There you are!" Zazu called from above as they got closer. He swooped down to scold the friends. "I've been looking for you two everywhere! Where have you been all day?"

"Sorry, Zazu," Simba said. "We were just looking for a cub-house."

"We found a bunch of cool places," Nala explained. "But Scar didn't want us around, we almost got crushed at the watering hole, and, well—"

"We didn't find it yet . . . but we will!" Simba said. "For now, we're ready to go home."

At Pride Rock, Simba cuddled up with Sarabi. "You know what, Mom?" Simba said as he tried to settle down. "I still want to find the perfect cubhouse someday, but for now it's good to be home."

"Ah, yes. That's because you belong here," Sarabi whispered to her son. "And no matter where your adventures lead you, you will always have a place in my heart."

Hustle Up

Long before he met Judy Hopps, Nick Wilde was a street-smart fox.

But one day Nick placed a bet against Mr. Big and lost.

"You have six hours to get me the money you owe, Nicky.

Otherwise"—Mr. Big gazed upon a deep pit of ice—"you're iced."

Nick was hurrying downtown when he spotted a little old bat trying to park her huge van. If only Nick could get that van! He could sell it to pay Mr. Big.

Nick approached her and offered to carry her groceries to her apartment. He told her he worked for Fur-Less Foxes, a charity that provided fur implants for the mange afflicted. "Why don't you donate the van to my charity, take the tax credit, and buy something more your size?"

She agreed and handed over the keys. His plan had worked!

But when he got to the van, his worst enemy, Finnick, had already hot-wired it and was behind the wheel driving off.

Lately, every time he turned around, Finnick was there.

If there was one hustler in all of Zootopia Nick wished would go away, it was Finnick.

"Au revoir, bug brain!" he said, in his deep, gravelly voice. Then he zoomed away.

But Nick shook it off. He had plenty of great ideas. *In fact, I have more great ideas in one day than Finnick will have in his whole life,* Nick thought. Nick would get the money some other way.

When he saw Big Al's Fine Cars, his eyes lit up. He grabbed a discarded trench coat off a bus bench and slipped it on. Nick entered the dealership and wandered toward the mouse cars. He stuffed some of the tiny vehicles into his pockets and sauntered out.

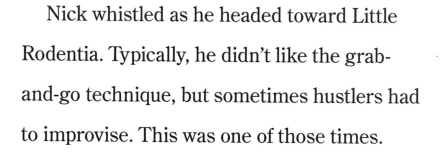

Nick whistled as he headed toward Little Rodentia. Typically, he didn't like the grab-and-go technique, but sometimes hustlers had to improvise. This was one of those times.

He set a blue convertible car down for a mouse to check out. "And it's yours for a grand."

"I have the same model for nine hundred fifty dollars!" came a gruff voice from the other end of the alley.

It was Finnick! The mouse headed toward Nick's rival.

"Nine hundred dollars," Nick said, narrowing his eyes at Finnick.

"Seven hundred!" said Finnick.

"You can have this one for six hundred dollars, and it runs like a dream!" said Nick.

"Two hundred dollars!" shouted Finnick. "Plus a free wash!"

"One hundred seventy-five dollars final," Nick countered.

"Zero!" said Finnick, rolling the car toward the mouse.

"Yes!" the mouse said. He jumped in and took off.

Suddenly, a stretch limo pulled up, and two polar bears stepped out.

Then they opened a door to reveal . . . Mr. Big!

"Time's up," he said. "I'm here to collect what you both owe me."

Finnick owes Mr. Big, too? Nick thought.

But neither Nick nor Finnick had the money.

"Ice 'em!" Mr. Big ordered.

As the polar bears reached for the two hustlers, Nick had an idea.

"Uh, um . . . Mr. Big," he said. "Sir . . . oh, honorable . . . one. Give us until sundown."

"You know I can't do that, Nicky—"

"We'll double the money we owe," said Nick, crossing his arms with confidence.

Finnick looked at Nick, confused, while Mr. Big considered the offer.

"Okay," Mr. Big said. "I'll see you at sundown. And you'd better have it, or it's Ice Town for you both."

Nick nodded. "Yup. I know. We'll have it."

Mr. Big held out his hand.

Nick and Finnick eyed each other before they took turns kissing his little ring.

After the tiny crime lord
had left, Nick and Finnick
had to get to work, and Nick
already had a plan.

He instructed Finnick to
drive to a large recycling bin to
collect water bottles.

"What? The garbage?" asked
Finnick.

"It's not garbage," said Nick.
"It's opportunity. With my ideas
and your size, the money will
roll in!"

Once the van was full of
bottles, they headed for the
Rainforest District.

Nick and Finnick stood the bottles up and used the rainwater to fill them.

When the bottles were full, they got back into the van.

"All right," said Nick. "It's money time. Next stop: Sahara Square."

When they arrived at Sahara Square, Finnick disconnected a pipe on a water fountain.

"This is busted!" said a cub trying to get a drink.

"Fresh, cold, natural water," called Nick, holding up a bottle.

"We'll just buy some from this nice fox and his little boy," the cub's mother said.

Finnick forced a pained smile when Nick patted him on the head as Finnick accepted payment for the water.

Nick and Finnick sold water bottles all afternoon. When they had only a few left, Finnick went to get the van.

But Finnick never came back! Nick waited and waited. Where had Finnick gone? Had the van been towed? Had Finnick been hauled off to jail?

And he had the money with him!

Nick walked off. *When I find him I'm going to ice him myself,* Nick thought.

After an hour, Nick finally realized Finnick wasn't coming back. Nick started feeling nervous. He knew Mr. Big would be expecting his money at sundown.

Suddenly, Finnick pulled up.

"Where have you—" Nick started. But then he noticed the painting on the side of the van.

"If we're going to work together, we need a stylish vehicle."

"'Work together,' huh?" said Nick. "I knew you liked me."

Back in Tundratown, Nick and Finnick handed over the cash to Mr. Big and left as fast as they could.

"So, what are we doing tomorrow?" Finnick asked as they sped through the streets of downtown.

"I have an idea, *and* it's not even really that illegal," Nick said.

Finnick shrugged, turned up his French rap music, and put the pedal to the metal.

Back at home, Nick went for a stroll.

Tires screeched as a car zoomed

by him. It was the old bat—in a fancy new car.

"Thanks for the advice!" she said to Nick. "You were right: a car more

my size does suit me!"

Nick smiled as he watched her race off. His hustle had worked. And

with Finnick as his partner, even more opportunities awaited him.

A New
Reindeer Friend

PRINCESS ANNA AND QUEEN ELSA had been working hard to prepare for the kingdom's first ball since Elsa's magical powers were revealed. The people had accepted Elsa—and her magic—wholeheartedly, and the sisters wanted to thank them with a special celebration.

"I want the people of Arendelle to know we care," Elsa said. "I want this ball to be different from anything they've ever seen!"

"Oh, Elsa," said Anna, "just having a ball is special!"

"I agree, Your Majesty," said Gerda, entering the room. "Hmmm. Crocus flowers would be nice for the centerpieces though."

"That's true, but everything already looks beautiful," Anna said. "The party is tonight, Elsa, and you need a break. Besides, I want to spend some time with you!"

"I'd love to," replied Elsa. "But what about the crocuses?"

"Well," said Anna, thinking quickly, "let's gather the crocuses ourselves! We'll do something useful, and we'll spend time together."

When Anna saw Olaf heading toward them, she invited him to come along. "We're going to look for crocuses! Please come."

Olaf clapped his hands. "Oooh! I love crocuses!"

Anna, Elsa, and Olaf hiked into the mountains and played all day.

They enjoyed acting silly and having fun outside of the castle walls.

"Maybe our party should be a costume ball!" Anna giggled.

"That's right, the ball!" said Elsa. "Don't forget, we still need crocuses!"

As they made their way home, Anna spotted Wandering Oaken's Trading Post and Sauna. "Look!" cried Anna. "I bet Oaken will have something unusual for our ball."

She ran inside, pulling Elsa along behind her.

"Hoo hoo!" called Oaken as the girls entered the trading post.

"Hello! Do you have anything special for a ball?" asked Anna.

"My big winter blowout is special. Half off shoes for walking on snow!

Or sleds for sliding down mountains!" Oaken exclaimed.

Outside, Elsa looked at Anna, who had a new sled full of winter supplies. "Anna, we already did the winter in summer thing, remember? We were looking for crocuses."

Anna grinned. "I know, of course, but he was so nice, how could I say no?"

Elsa had to laugh.

As they set out again, Olaf ran ahead, shouting, "This is the best day of my life!"

Finally, they found the crocuses on a grassy peak. Elsa gasped.

"They're beautiful!"

While the girls collected flowers, Olaf chased a bee. All was well until . . .

"Hang on there, Olaf!" exclaimed Elsa, catching the snowman with her magic as he tumbled.

But Olaf didn't even notice. "Look at that!" he said, staring at something below. It was a young reindeer trapped on a ledge.

"How did you get down there?" Anna asked. "And how will we get you out?"

Elsa thought for a moment. Then she waved her hands. Suddenly, a ramp of ice sprang magically into existence, winding down to the ledge.

"Whoa," said Olaf. "Now the little reindeer can climb out!"

Carefully, the reindeer stepped onto the ramp . . .

but the ice was too slippery!

"Now what?" asked Elsa.

"I know!" said Anna. She jumped onto the ramp. Down she slid with her arms full of the supplies from Oaken's.

First Anna pulled out the snowshoes. "I knew these would be useful,"
she said, fitting them on the reindeer.

Then she tied a rope around the reindeer
and threw it to Elsa.

"Pull!" Anna shouted.

Even Olaf was able to help.

At last, everyone was safe at the top!

"Can we invite the reindeer to the ball?" asked Olaf.

"The ball!" Anna and Elsa shouted together.

Elsa grabbed Anna and Olaf's hands and led them to the sled. "Hold on!" she said. Using her magic, she created a series of snow slides that launched them down the mountain.

When the entire group finally arrived, they landed in the middle of the ballroom!

Crocus flowers rained down on the guests, who were delighted at the grand entrance.

"See?" said Anna. "Nobody has ever seen a ball like this before!"

Elsa laughed. "And best of all, we're together!"

A Delicious Duo

Alfredo Linguini walked into his restaurant one morning to the smell of a delicious mushroom-and-cheese omelet.

He entered the kitchen to find his friend Remy cooking up a wonderful breakfast for the two of them.

"What a great surprise. This looks really good!" Linguini said.

As they ate, Remy noticed his friend was quieter than usual.

"This surprise reminded me that today is Colette's birthday," Linguini said with a sigh. "And I have no idea what to get her. Maybe some flowers? Or, ah . . . a hat, or—"

Remy thought they could make Colette a nice meal for her birthday, so he picked up his favorite cookbook.

"Hey," Linguini said, seeing the book. "This gives me an idea. I can *cook* her something! I bet she'd love that!"

Remy sighed with relief, glad Linguini had figured out the same perfect birthday plan.

Linguini landed on a recipe he thought even
he could cook: *scoglio*, a seafood pasta.

Remy nodded and began running around
the kitchen collecting the ingredients they'd
need. Whatever he didn't find, Linguini
wrote on a list to take to the supermarket.

Linguini also added a note to get flowers.
Remy thought that idea was pretty good, too.

Once Linguini had the final list, he headed for the door. "Thanks for your help, Little Chef."

Remy jumped up on his ladder, ready to join Linguini.

"I really appreciate all your help," Linguini said, "but since this is a special gift from me to Colette, I think I, uh, I want to do this on my own."

But when he got to the supermarket, he saw there were ten ingredients needed . . . just for the pasta sauce! Linguini headed down the closest aisle and saw premade jars of pasta sauce. He knew Remy would never approve, but with so little time, he decided to grab a sauce and move on.

Next on the list were some vegetables. The cookbook instructions had listed detailed steps for chopping and dicing and spiralizing, so he was happy to find a freezer full of precut veggies.

After the supermarket, Linguini headed for the fish market and flower stand by the river.

The list said to buy fresh fish, like mussels, scallops, or shrimp. But Linguini spotted a sign advertising live lobsters. *That's as fresh as fish can get!* Linguini thought. He bought the largest lobster at the fish market, quickly grabbed a bouquet of flowers, and was on his way!

When Linguini returned to the restaurant, Remy was shocked to see that he'd hardly followed the list at all!

But Remy knew that a good chef could make a great meal out of any ingredients, so he hopped up on the counter and began to revise the dinner plan.

"Whoa, what are you doing?" Linguini asked. "I've got it from here. Why don't you sit down and, uh, relax?"

Half an hour into cooking, Linguini was a little surprised everything was going so smoothly—until he turned around to see Remy testing the sauce. "Little Chef!" Linguini exclaimed. "I know you're just trying to help, but

I really want to do this by myself. You know? I just want to try."

Remy understood. Linguini was trying to do something from the heart, and Remy wanted to let his friend do just that.

With Remy gone, Linguini tried his best to pay extra-close attention to what he was doing . . . but things quickly fell apart.

Just when Linguini thought things couldn't get any worse, the sauce exploded all over the kitchen!

Linguini sank to the floor and called for his friend. "Little Chef!"

Remy ran into the kitchen and sat down next to Linguini.

"I'm sorry, pal," Linguini said. "I wanted this gift to be from me to her, but I think we'll create something even more special together. Would you help me finish cooking? Colette deserves a great meal on her birthday, and I know with your help we can make one."

Remy got up and began running around the kitchen. Then he started
flipping through the cookbook, searching for a different recipe.

Eventually, Remy found something they could make together using
what Linguini had left from the store and what Remy had in the restaurant.

Remy hopped on Linguini's head to get to work.

Just as they finished cooking, Colette arrived.

Linguini led her to a table. "Linguini by Linguini . . . and Little Chef!" he announced.

"This food smells amazing!" she exclaimed, smiling. "How'd you know this was my favorite pasta? And flowers, too!"

Linguini and Remy shared a knowing look.

"I had a bit of help." Linguini chuckled. "Happy birthday, Colette."

It Takes Two

"We did it!" Mowgli hollered.

He had just escaped from King Louie and the monkeys with his friends Baloo and Bagheera.

"It sure was a swinging good time," Baloo said.

Bagheera was less enthusiastic. "Next time, we need to stick to the plan! We're lucky to be alive."

"We need to find a safe place for the night," Bagheera said. "King Louie may still be after Mowgli."

"Aw, loosen up!" Baloo said. "I can protect us. If we see any of those mangy monkeys, I'll jab with my left, and I'll swing with my right—"

"Oh, Baloo. We need to protect the boy. Think about it," Bagheera said.

Mowgli sighed. He didn't need protecting. Why, with his brawn he could fight like a bear. And with his brains he could plan like a panther . . . if only they'd give him the chance!

Just then Mowgli heard something.

There was a rustling sound above his head, in the trees.

Mowgli giggled as a flying squirrel glided above him and landed on a branch. "I want to try that!" he shouted.

Mowgli climbed a tree and grabbed a vine. But try as he might, he just kept crashing to the ground.

Finally, Mowgli got the hang of it. He felt like he was flying! He and the squirrel swept over the heads of Bagheera and Baloo. Mowgli was having the time of his life, but soon his stomach started grumbling. "There are some bananas!" he told the squirrel, pointing across the river. "Let's race!"

There was just one problem: Mowgli and his new friend didn't know how to cross the river.

Mowgli looked at the vine he was holding and got an idea.

"Let's swing," Mowgli said. "On the count of three: one, two, *three*!"

"*Eeeeeep!*" the squirrel shrieked.

Mowgli swung across the water. But his hands slipped, and he fell into the river.

Kaa, the snake, had been watching Mowgli and happened to be a very good swimmer. He was waiting for his prey on the other side of the river.

"Oh, there'sssss the Man-cub, ssssswinging to me," he said. This was his chance to get the Man-cub!

Kaa slithered down from his tree and his eyes grew wide. "Trussssst in me," he told Mowgli. "Jusssst sssslide into my coils."

Mowgli and the squirrel grabbed on to Kaa, who pulled them up into the tree with him.

"Oh, look. A sssssquirrel," Kaa hissed, slithering even closer.

The squirrel's eyes focused on Kaa. Soon he had fallen under Kaa's spell.

Using his brain,
Mowgli realized that
if he didn't look
into Kaa's eyes,
the snake could
not make him go to
sleep. And using his brawn,
Mowgli wrapped Kaa's tail around a stone and pushed it down a hill.

The snake fell from the tree.

"Ssssome thankssss I get!" Kaa muttered.

"Mowgli!"

"Little Britches!"

Bagheera and Baloo stood across the river, shouting. They had been worried about Mowgli since he ran off. King Louie might still be out there looking for him, and Baloo and Bagheera wanted to keep him safe.

"I'm over here!" Mowgli hollered. "I used my brains and my brawn to save—"

"What? We can't hear you!" said Baloo.

Mowgli turned to look at his new friend. "Thanks for teaching me how to glide! I hope we meet again," he said. "Maybe next time I'll try gliding *without* the vine."

The squirrel chittered at Mowgli and then flew away, high above the ground.

"Hmmm," Mowgli said, watching the squirrel take flight. "Maybe that's not such a good idea after all."

Mowgli made his way downriver, past the waterfalls.

On the other side of the river, Bagheera and Baloo followed him. When he reached a patch of calm water, Mowgli swung—and swam—to his friends.

Mowgli threw himself into Baloo's arms. He'd had a fun adventure, but he was glad to be back safe and sound.

That night, as Mowgli drifted off to sleep, he heard his friends still arguing.

"He used brains. He didn't look into Kaa's eyes," Bagheera said.

"It was brawn! He used a big rock to get rid of Kaa," Baloo argued.

Mowgli smiled. He had used his brains *and* his brawn to save himself and his new friend!

Donald Duck
and the **Dairy Farm**

Early one summer morning, Mickey Mouse, Donald Duck, and Donald's nephews arrived at Grandma Duck's farm. They had promised to take care of Grandma's cows while she was on vacation.

Mickey and the boys found the cows drinking from a pond. Mickey, Huey, Dewey, and Louie led them into the barn. But one cow would not move. She was standing behind a big round bale of hay.

"Here, cow! Here, cow!" Donald called.

Mickey and the boys hurried over to see what was happening. Next to the cow stood a little calf.

"This must be Rosie and her new calf!" Mickey said. "We're supposed to take the calf to the barn and help it drink from a bottle."

Donald tried to lead the calf to the barn, but Rosie blocked his way. He tried to push Rosie aside, but she pushed him back. Soon Rosie was chasing Donald around the pasture.

Meanwhile, Mickey, Huey, Dewey, and Louie led the calf inside and fed it.

Suddenly, Donald dashed into a milking stall, with Rosie close behind him. Donald slipped away from the cow, slammed the stall door shut, and leaned against it.

"Guess I showed her who's boss!"

he said, wiping his forehead.

Donald watched as Mickey and the boys attached the other cows to the milking machines.

"That looks easy," he said. But when he tried it with Rosie, she pushed him over and started to run. "Whoa!" Donald shouted, grabbing her tail.

As Rosie dragged Donald through the barn, his feet got tangled in the hoses that carried milk to the storage tank.

Snap! One of the hoses came loose.

Milk sprayed everywhere, soaking Donald from head to toe and splashing in his eyes.

Donald stumbled over hoses and milk cans and bumped into doors. Finally, he put his foot straight into a bucket, tripped, and fell into a feed bin.

"Oof!" Donald gasped as he climbed out, covered with bits of mashed grain. "That's it!"

Donald grabbed an old milking stool and a

bucket and marched toward Rosie.

"I'm going to milk this cow the old-fashioned

way—by hand!"

When Rosie saw Donald approaching, a sly glint came into her eyes. As soon as he got close enough, she gave him a powerful kick and sent him flying through the air.

Splash! Donald landed headfirst in a full can of milk.

Mickey pulled Donald out of the can. "I think you've helped enough for today," he said. "We'll finish milking Rosie."

Mickey calmly milked the cow, and then the boys put her in a stall with her calf. After their chores were done, the gang trooped back to the house for a rest.

Just then, Grandma Duck drove up. "I missed my cows too much to go away," she said.

"Hmph! I hope I never see another cow again," Donald said.

"Hmmm," Grandma said, handing out gifts to everyone. "That's too bad."

Mickey opened his box, and everyone began to laugh—even Donald.

Inside was a huge piece of chocolate, and it was shaped just like a cow!

Winnie the Pooh

Who Cares?
Pooh Cares!

One bright and cheery day in the Hundred-Acre Wood, a mama duck waited patiently for her eggs to hatch.

Suddenly, three fuzzy yellow ducklings poked through their spotted shells.

Mama Duck greeted them with a loud and proud "Quaaaack!"

She then led her ducklings to the pond for their first swimming lesson.

But Mama Duck didn't notice that one spotted egg was left behind. When the tiny duckling poked out from his shell, he began to quack softly for his mama. But there was no answer, so he sat and waited . . . and waited . . . and waited.

Now on this very same day in the Hundred-Acre Wood, Winnie the Pooh and his best friend, Piglet, decided to go for a morning stroll.

It wasn't long before Piglet's ears perked up. "Pooh," he said. "Do you hear something?"

Pooh listened carefully. "I believe I do," he answered.

Pooh parted some lilies to discover a tiny fuzzy duckling sitting there.

"We must find his mother!" said Pooh.

So the two friends gently nudged the duckling out of his nest and went

off to search. But there were no ducks in sight.

"There's only one thing to do now," said Pooh. "We shall take him to

my house."

"Before we do," said Piglet, "this little duckling needs a name."

"Oh, yes," Pooh agreed. "And I think you just named him."

"I did?" asked Piglet. "Funny, I don't remember. . . ."

"Little," said Pooh. "That's what we'll call him. Because he is so very that!"

"Follow us, Little!" said Piglet with a giggle. "We are taking you to Pooh's house."

At Pooh's house, the friends found a small box to make into a comfy bed for Little.

Pooh let the duckling borrow a blanket so he'd be nice and cozy, and Piglet set up a night-light in case he was afraid of the dark.

Then Piglet filled a saucer with water and left it next to Little's new bed. "Just in case he gets thirsty," he said.

The next morning, Pooh, Piglet, and Little went to visit Rabbit for their first meal of the day.

"We were wondering if you might have a little something for him to eat," Pooh said.

Exactly one minute later, Rabbit presented Little with a plate of tiny green beans, peas, and half a chopped tomato.

After breakfast, Pooh and Piglet took Little
to Kanga and Roo's house.

"Oh, boy, Mama," said Roo. "I have a new
friend! I'm going to teach him all my games!"

The first game was follow-the-leader.
After a while, Roo moved on to
playing hide-and-seek.

Soon after, Little was in for something
special. For there was nothing Roo loved more
than making pies from soft, squishy mud.

After a bath and a snack, Pooh, Piglet, and Little headed home and stopped to visit Owl on the way.

"Well, bust my beak, aren't you something!" pronounced Owl. "Let me show you how to primp and plump those fuzzy yellow feathers of yours, dear fellow!"

After saying goodbye and thanking Owl, a fuller, fluffier Little waddled home with Winnie the Pooh.

The very next day, Tigger and Roo came to Pooh's house to give Little a bouncing lesson.

"Hoo-hoo-hoo!" cried Tigger. "Let's bounce to the pond and take you for a swim, li'l Little!

So Little got his first lesson in bouncing, which, for him, was more like a long waddle followed by two quick hops.

At the pond, Roo introduced Little to the most amazing creatures!

Little took a ride on the back of a turtle, splashed with a playful perch, and bounced with a croaking frog.

"I think he likes it here," said Roo. After their swim, Tigger bounced Roo and Little home.

The next day, after a good night's sleep, Eeyore came by to show Little his home and to ask Little if he could teach him how to waddle.

Little nodded willingly and began to waddle around the thistle patch. Then Eeyore began to waddle, too! He waddled up; he waddled back; he waddled left; he waddled right . . . then he tipped right over!

"I knew it was too good to last," said Eeyore.

When it was time to leave, Eeyore walked Little to Pooh's house. But before long, he realized they were lost.

"Better just sit tight and wait for somebody to come and find us," Eeyore said.

Eeyore and Little nestled together and took a little nap while they waited to be found. After what seemed like a very long while, Pooh and Piglet found them fast asleep beneath a willow tree.

Together, the friends walked
and waddled home to
Pooh's house.

When Pooh and
Piglet put Little to
bed, they heard the
duckling quacking
in his sleep.

"Listen, Pooh,"
said Piglet. "I think
he's quacking,
'Maaa-maaaa,
Maaa-maaa.'"

"Oh, dear," said
Pooh. "Perhaps it's time
to try and find Little's mother again."

The next day, after taking Little to Kanga's house, Pooh and Piglet found Mama Duck! After quite a lot of talking and clapping and quacking, Pooh and Piglet got her to accompany them to Kanga's house. And there followed a heartwarming reunion between Little and his mama.

"I will miss Little," Pooh said to his friends, "but I'm happy that he is going to be with his family now. And he'll always be welcome here."

DUMBO

Timothy's Big Day

Timothy Q. Mouse looked out over the edge of Dumbo's hat and grinned. Below him, the crowd cheered for the flying elephant.

Timothy loved the circus. There was no place in the world he would rather be.

Later that night, Timothy watched the crew pack up the circus. It was time to move on to a new town. But first the Ringmaster had to pass out letters and packages to the performers.

Unseen by the Ringmaster, a tiny envelope fell out of his pile.

Timothy scurried over to the fallen letter. The mouse turned the envelope over to see who it was for and then gasped. It was for him!

221

Timothy couldn't believe it. His family was coming to see him! He hadn't spoken to them since he'd left home to join the circus. To his parents, life on the farm was perfect. They couldn't imagine living anywhere else.

Timothy hurried over to Dumbo's stall.

"Oh, boy. Look at this, will ya?" Timothy shouted, waving around the letter. "My parents are coming to see you perform, Dumbo. We'll put on such a show for them, they'll *have* to like the circus. After all, who wouldn't love a flying elephant?"

As the circus traveled to the next town, Timothy grew more and more excited about seeing his parents.

But Timothy was nervous, too. What if his parents didn't think he'd done a good job with Dumbo after all? He wanted them to be proud of him. And that meant he *had* to show them how great circus life was.

The next morning, the circus train pulled into the station. After so long away, Timothy felt strange to know that he was home again.

He wondered if he would see his family in the crowd. But there were too many people. If the mice had come, there was no way he'd be able to find them.

Finally, the animals arrived at the circus site. Timothy watched as the circus hands got to work setting up the big top. No matter how many times he saw it, watching the tent go up never got any less exciting.

"Just wait until my family gets a load of this," Timothy said to Dumbo. "The lights. The noise. And you, Dumbo. I can't wait for them to see your act."

But at that moment, Dumbo let out a great big sneeze.

Dumbo sneezed again. And again.

"Oh, no," the Ringmaster said, hurrying over to look at the little elephant. "This is no good. You can't go on with a cold, and we can't go on without you."

The Ringmaster turned to the circus hands. "Sorry, lads. This fella needs his rest. Today's show will have to wait."

Timothy looked over at Dumbo. The Ringmaster was right: the little elephant did not look good at all.

"It's my job to take care of you, Dumbo," Timothy said with determination. "Let's find you somewhere comfortable to lie down."

Timothy led Dumbo to a cozy pile of hay and went to get a steaming bowl of peanut soup.

228

Then Timothy started to give Dumbo a warm bath, but Dumbo sneezed again.

Next the mouse found the warmest blanket he could and draped it over Dumbo. But it was no use. The elephant just kept sneezing.

"Well, the least I can do is make sure you get some peace and quiet so you can rest," Timothy said, moving to the front of the tent.

He felt bad for Dumbo. It was no fun to be sick. But he felt bad for himself, too. This was his chance to make his parents proud of him.

Timothy was still feeling sorry for himself a few hours later when he heard a familiar voice. "Timothy, dear. We have been looking for you everywhere!"

Timothy turned to see his mother, his father, and his brothers and sisters standing in front of him.

"Mother. Father. You're here." The little mouse hung his head. "I'm afraid Dumbo has a cold. He can't go on tonight. I'm sorry you wasted your time coming."

"Wasted our time?" Timothy's father asked. "We came to the circus to see *you*. We're not big-city travelers but we're certainly not going to miss a chance to see our son!"

"You don't think I made a mistake joining the circus?" Timothy asked.

"There's no such thing as a mistake as long as you're doing what you love," his mother said.

At that moment, the flaps to Dumbo's tent rustled, and the little elephant stepped through, looking like he felt much better.

"Dumbo, old pal," Timothy said, "may I introduce you to my family?"

Dumbo was very pleased to meet them.

"If you'll excuse me," Timothy said to everyone, "I'd better let the Ringmaster know that Dumbo is feeling better." Then he turned to his parents. "Wait here, you two. I have something I'd like to show you."

That night, as Dumbo prepared to take to the air, Timothy climbed into his usual spot on the elephant's hat. But this time, he wasn't alone. Beside him were his parents.

With a great flapping of his ears, Dumbo lifted off the ground and soared over the circus crowd. Cheers filled the room at the sight of the flying elephant.

Who Needs a Hug?

Dory darted across the sandy floor in front of her parents' home in Morro Bay.

"It's our last day in Morro Bay," said Jenny, sighing. "I hope our new home will have lots of purple shells."

Dory couldn't wait to show off the reef and her coral cave to her mom and dad. And they couldn't wait to move in.

"I'm so happy we're together," said Jenny. "I think I need a hug. A great big oh-so-tight family hug."

"You know who gives great hugs?" Dory asked. "Nemo! I wonder what he's up to. I'd better go find him."

Dory swam through the dark green kelp and spied Nemo playing hide-and-seek with two new friends.

"Found you both!" a parrot fish called to his friends.

"Oh, no!" cried Nemo, laughing.

"Hey, what's wrong with your fin?" their other friend, an angelfish, asked Nemo. "It's so tiny."

Nemo looked at his fin. He didn't think it looked wrong.

Dory swam down from the kelp. "That tiny fin took Nemo across the entire Pacific Ocean," she said. "He's one of the best swimmers I know. I think you need a hug, you super-duper swimmer."

"Er, not so tight," said Nemo. "Come play with us, Dory! You're it. Start counting!"

Dory started to count. But soon she noticed some shells and started counting them instead. She bumped into a giant stalk of kelp and saw something wriggling near the surface. Dory swam closer to get a better look. She spotted a small ball of fur looking down at her.

"Well, hello there!" Dory said to the ball of fur.

Meanwhile, Nemo and his friends waited for Dory to find them. They waited and waited and waited.

"I think Dory forgot about us," Nemo said. "We should go find her."

The three fish swam out from their hiding spots and found Dory. She was staring at something up in the kelp.

"Look! It's a baby otter," said the angelfish.

"He's so cute," said the parrot fish. "I just want to give him a hug!"

"Yay! One more player!" shouted Nemo. "Let's hide! Don't forget, Dory. You need to look for us!"

Nemo and his friends swam off again. The otter pup wriggled out of the seaweed. He dove and splashed in the water. He couldn't wait to hide.

Dory began to count. "Ten, nine, eight . . . twelve, eleven, ten . . . three, two, one . . . Ready or not, here I come!"

Dory darted this way and that way.

She found Nemo. He was hiding in a group of sea urchins. Then she found the angelfish and parrot fish. They were hiding behind some rocks.

"My turn! It's my turn to hide!" Dory shouted.

Nemo looked around. "But where's the otter?" he asked. "Did you find him?"

"Oh, that cute little brown ball of fur . . . well . . . um . . . no," Dory admitted.

"Bet he found the *best* hiding spot," the angelfish whispered to the parrot fish.

They looked and looked but couldn't find him anywhere.

"If he's lost, you can find him, Dory," Nemo said. "When I was lost, you helped my dad find me."

"You can count on me," said Dory as she darted off to find the otter.

Nemo and his friends raced after her. They swam under a tall red buoy and around a large gray rock.

"Look!" Dory shouted. "Over there—that looks like an otter. Swim this way!"

But it wasn't the little otter. It was Destiny and Bailey. When Destiny saw Dory, she suddenly bumped into something soft and squishy, and a cloud of black ink crept into the water.

"Oh, no," gasped Bailey. "It's Hank."

Hank blushed and slunk down to hide. Destiny swam over to console him.

"I'm sorry, Hank," whispered Destiny. "I didn't mean to scare you. Do you need a hug?"

"Me? Hug? Nah," grumbled Hank as he pushed Destiny away.

"Hank's worried about looking silly," explained Nemo. "But accidents happen to all of us."

"I get a little embarrassed when I bump into things," admitted Destiny. "I'm not a great swimmer."

"Yes, you are!" Dory assured her friend. "You swim beautifully."

"Awww, thank you!" Destiny said.

"Let's go," said Nemo. "We need to find the otter and get him safely back home before his parents worry."

"Can I help?" asked Destiny.

"Ooh-ooh! Me too!" shouted Bailey.

Dory asked Bailey to use his echolocation to help find the otter.

Bailey put his flippers to his head.

"OOOOOOOOOOO. I think it's working," he said. "He's in the kelp forest. Go straight and then left."

"Excellent work, Bailey!" said Dory as she gave his flipper a quick squeeze.

Even Hank agreed to help look. "I think I found the otter over here," he
called to his friends. And there the little otter was . . . sound asleep on a
kelp bed.

"Awww," sighed Dory. "Poor little guy probably got tired of waiting to be
found and fell asleep. Let's get him back home."

Destiny slowly glided upward and gently lifted the sleeping otter out of
the water.

Bailey swam ahead to guide Destiny as she carried the otter pup closer to shore.

"Go right, then left, Destiny," Bailey called out as he navigated around a rock.

Otters were everywhere! Some were chasing each other in the water. Some were diving for food. And a few were dozing on their backs.

The familiar sounds woke up the otter pup. He yawned, rubbed his furry face, and looked around. He squealed excitedly and jumped into the water.

Dory saw two otters waving from the rocks.

"Those must be his parents!" she said.

The little otter and his parents embraced in a huge otter family hug. They had missed their otter pup!

When the sun began to set over the bay, all the otters moved in closer and closer. One by one, they placed their arms around each other and began to hug. It was a giant cuddle party.

"That's one big happy family," said Hank.

Dory sighed. She remembered how much she loved her friends and family.

"I think I need a hug," she said.

Everyone—even Hank—gathered around Dory. They placed their fins, flippers, and arms around her and hugged. A little closer. A little tighter.

Lady and the TRAMP

Barking Up the Right Tree

"What a day!" Tramp said, gazing out the window into the garden. "C'mon! What are we waitin' for? Let's go outside and do something fun!" he called to Lady.

Lady jumped up from her cozy cushion and happily padded toward the doggy door. "Why don't we play hide-and-seek?" she suggested.

"That's a swell idea," said Tramp. "Last one outside is it!"

A few minutes later, Tramp was busy counting. "Seven . . . eight . . . nine . . . ten! Ready or not, here I come!" he said.

Tramp opened his eyes and quickly scanned the garden. He looked right. He looked left. He looked up *and* down. Finally, he saw them: two dainty pale-brown paws peeking out from beneath the flowers!

"Gotcha!" Tramp said, playfully pouncing paws-first into the flowers.

"Me-*ow*!"

"Hey!" Tramp cried. The next thing he knew, a blur of brown-and-white fur was hurtling past him.

"What was *that*?" Lady gasped, jumping out from behind the doghouse, where she had been hiding.

Tramp pointed to the thick trunk of the shady old elm tree. A fluffy brown-and-white kitten was racing straight up to the nearest branch.

"Oh, poor thing," Lady cooed. "You must have scared her, Tramp."

"Scared *her*?" Tramp frowned, shaking the thorns out of his tail. "More like she scared *me*!"

"Oh, Tramp," said Lady. "Don't tell me a little kitten scared you. It's all right," she called up to the kitten. "Tramp was only playing. We're sorry if you're frightened. Trust me, we'd never hurt you. It's perfectly safe to come back down."

The kitten peered at them from her branch, looking scared.

"Oh, won't you please come down?" Lady urged her.

But the kitten didn't move.

"Aw, shucks. Lemme talk to her," said Tramp, stretching up to rest his front paws against the tree. "Here, kitty," he called. "C'mon down. I'm sorry. I know I can seem a little, uh, big and scary, but really, we were just playing a game of hide-and-seek. If you come down, maybe you can play with us."

At last, the kitten moved, but only to tiptoe farther along the branch.

"Looks like she's happy up there," Tramp said, shrugging.

"Or maybe she's stuck!" Lady said. "Oh, Tramp, we have to help her!"

Tramp didn't have much interest in helping the kitten out of the tree, but he would do anything for Lady. And Lady had a plan—a plan that seemed like it just might work *if* he helped her.

"You stand here, next to the tree, and let me climb on your back," Lady told Tramp. "Then, maybe, if I stretch as far as I can, I can reach that kitten."

As it so happened, at that very moment, Jock was strolling by the garden and decided to drop by.

"Well, I must say! This is a grand sight!" he exclaimed as he spotted Tramp and Lady. "You certainly don't see somethin' like this every day, now do you? Would this be a new trick Darling and Jim Dear taught you?"

"Oh, no. It's no trick,"
Lady told Jock. She
explained that she and
Tramp were trying to help
the kitten down from the
tree. "Unfortunately, I can't
get high enough," Lady said.

"Aye, I can see that, lass,"
Jock replied.

"Maybe if you climbed up
and stood on me . . ." Lady
began.

"Say no more!" Jock
gallantly told her. "As
ever, my lady, I am at your
service!"

A few minutes later, Trusty wandered over from his front porch. "Well, I do declare," he said, even more surprised than Jock had been. "Miss Lady, what in the world are you and Jock doing up *there*?"

Lady explained the situation. "I see, I see," Trusty said.

"Unfortunately," sighed Lady, "we still can't reach the kitten. But maybe if *you* helped us, Trusty . . ."

"Why, Miss Lady," replied Trusty, "what kind of gentleman would I be if I didn't oblige such a request?"

Carefully, everyone climbed down. Then Tramp climbed onto Trusty's back, and Lady and Jock climbed back into place.

"Can you reach the branch now, Jock?" Lady called up to him.

"Aye!" said Jock, wagging his tail.

"Awoo!" howled Trusty, so happy that he didn't notice the butterfly landing on his nose . . . until it was too late.

Suddenly, Trusty's howl turned into a howling sneeze!

Before the dogs knew it, their hard-fought tower had collapsed into a furry, twelve-legged pile.

Twelve legs? Lady counted again. *Shouldn't there be sixteen legs?* she thought. "Where's Jock?" she asked.

"Up here, lassie!"

Lady looked up, along with Tramp and Trusty, to see Jock dangling by his front paws from the branch.

"I don't suppose you could get back up here in a hurry," Jock called down as calmly as he could. "I'm having a wee bit of trouble holding on."

Quickly, the dogs re-formed their tower. At the bottom, Trusty kept an eye out for any butterflies, determined to hold his ground this time. At the top, Jock regained his footing on Lady's shoulders.

"Here, kitty, kitty . . ." he said. "Here—"

"Is something wrong?" Lady asked when Jock suddenly stopped.

"Aye," Jock answered her, looking up and down the branch. "There is one wee problem, I'm afraid."

The kitten was not on the branch anymore. In fact, the kitten wasn't even in the tree!

"Why, I do declare!" Trusty exclaimed, looking down. "If that li'l ol' kitten ain't a-rubbin' my back leg!"

"Aye, so she is!" Jock said.

"Oh, how wonderful," Lady said.

"You've gotta be kidding me," Tramp groaned.

"I just love happy endings, don't you?" Lady asked when everyone was back on the ground.

Jock and Trusty agreed.

"Yeah, they're okay, I guess," Tramp said as the kitten took a turn around his leg. "But you know what I like even better?"

"What?" Lady asked.

"Playing hide-and seek! Hey, kitten! You're it!"

Bath Time for Lucifer

$\mathcal{T}$he morning sun shone through the windows of the
Tremaine manor. Cinderella stood in her stepsister Anastasia's
room, listening to that day's list of chores.

"Make sure our dresses are mended for the garden party," Anastasia
was saying.

"And pressed!" Cinderella's other stepsister, Drizella, added.

The sound of footsteps behind
her made Cinderella turn around.

"I have a few little tasks for you,
as well," said her stepmother, Lady
Tremaine. Washing, sewing, dusting,
mopping—the list seemed to go
on forever!

Cinderella looked down at the
floor, trying to remember all that
she had to do, and she noticed
Lucifer the cat slinking around.

"Oh, yes," Lady Tremaine added.
"Do make sure that Lucifer gets
a bath."

With that, Cinderella's stepmother
swept off down the hall.

Lucifer had heard the word *bath* . . . and he didn't like the idea one bit.

Once Cinderella took a step toward him, he sprang to his feet and ran out of Anastasia's bedroom as fast as his paws could carry him. Cinderella knew that *catch Lucifer* would have to go before *bathe Lucifer* on her long list of things to do that day.

But Lucifer had no intention of being caught . . . or bathed. He would need to hide. Looking around, he saw a big vase on a table. Lucifer tried to climb up, but the vase came tumbling down.

Cinderella heard the sound of the vase thumping to the ground and Lucifer's unhappy meow. When she went to pick up the vase, Lucifer vanished again.

"You okay, Cinderelly?" came a small voice from under the table.

Cinderella looked down to see two of her little mouse friends, Gus and Jaq.

"I have to give Lucifer a bath," Cinderella explained, "and I'm pretty certain he's trying to hide from me, but if I spend all day looking for him, I'll never get my other chores done."

"We help!" Jaq said immediately, nudging Gus, who nodded. "We look for Lucifee!"

Gus and Jaq went to Cinderella's room to tell the birds and mice that Cinderella needed all their help.

Suzy, Perla, and the other mice would help with Cinderella's chores, at least the mouse-sized ones.

The birds agreed to spread the word to the other animals to see if anyone had spotted Lucifer.

Meanwhile, upstairs, Lucifer thought he had found the perfect hiding spot: a warm, sunny patch behind the curtains in the music room.

But it wasn't long before he was disturbed by a terrible noise— Anastasia and Drizella's music lesson!

Lucifer couldn't stand it, and he burst from behind the curtains and out of the music room.

Fleeing downstairs, Lucifer found himself in the kitchen, but he could already hear voices in the hallway nearby. Thinking quickly, he jumped into a pail and curled up in a ball.

Right after he had hidden, Gus and Jaq entered the room to search for him.

Lucifer tried his best to hold very still, but he couldn't resist the idea of chasing the mice. He sprang out of the pail, but his foot caught on the handle, knocking it over with a dreadful clatter.

"We have to tell Cinderelly we found him!" Jaq said.

Hearing the mice call for her, Cinderella ran into the kitchen.

But Lucifer was already getting back to his feet. He fled out the door to the barn and hid in the rafters of the stable—a very promising hiding place, he thought, swishing his tail happily.

Unfortunately for him, his tail swished some hay off the rafter—straight onto the nose of Major the horse. Like the other animals, Major had heard that Lucifer was hiding from Cinderella. He whinnied an alert.

Lucifer darted between Major's hooves and ran straight for the forest, not even looking where he was going. He kept running until he couldn't run anymore.

When he looked up, Lucifer had no idea where he was.

At first that seemed like a good thing. He could stay lost until he was ready to go home, which he hoped would be long after Cinderella had given up on the idea of giving him a bath.

Lucifer thought it seemed like a marvelous plan . . . until thunder started to roll. The dark day was about to become a stormy afternoon.

Cinderella was getting concerned as the rain began to fall. She tied a scarf over her hair and picked up a lantern.

"Where you going, Cinderelly?" Gus asked.

"To find Lucifer," Cinderella said. "While Lucifer may not be the nicest cat, no one deserves to be out in this weather. And everyone deserves to have someone care about them."

She pushed the kitchen door open and headed out into the storm.

Soon Lucifer's paws were caked in mud, and his fur dragged in it, too. Even a bath would be better than this!

He was so busy feeling miserable that at first he didn't see the lantern shining through the trees, or hear Cinderella's call. "Lucifer? Oh, Lucifer!"

Lucifer was very ready to go home. He stepped out from under the bush, allowing Cinderella to pick him up. She was glad she'd found him in one piece.

Cinderella made sure to thank everyone for helping her find Lucifer and for the help with her chores.

In the bathroom, the tub was filled with water that was perfectly warm and wonderful, and the soap was scented with sweet flowers.

Lucifer still hated it. But he'd learned that baths weren't the worst thing after all—rain was much, much worse.

Thumper Finds a Friend

Under the warm, bright summer sun, Thumper and his sisters played tag in the forest.

Daisy chased after Trixie, who tried to wriggle away while Ria ducked behind a tree and Tessie giggled in her hiding spot. Thumper dove for cover behind a bush . . . and discovered someone who was trying not to be found.

It was a little hedgehog asleep in the nook of a tree.

The hedgehog awoke suddenly and was surprised to see Thumper standing there before her.

"Hello!" Thumper said. "Want to play tag with me and my sisters? It's really fun! Right now, we're all trying not to get tagged by my sister Daisy."

Thumper's sisters heard him talking to someone and hopped over to see who it was. But they accidentally startled the hedgehog even more!

She stumbled and tumbled and fell backward. Then she tucked her head down and rolled herself into a prickly little ball.

She didn't answer them.

Thumper tried again. "Hello, little hedgehog. Do you want to play tag with me and my sisters?"

But still no answer.

Does she not want to play tag? Maybe she doesn't know how, Thumper thought. He was completely puzzled. *Or maybe she doesn't want to be my friend.*

"Maybe I can make her laugh," Thumper said to his sisters and their forest friends. "Then she'll know we're friendly bunnies." He looked for something soft and tickly and found a feather nearby. "This'll work!" he cheered.

Flick, flick, feather-flick.

The hedgehog giggled. Thumper's plan had worked!

"Now do you want to play tag with us?" Thumper asked.

But still no answer from the little hedgehog.

Then Thumper had another idea! He would give her something sweet.
He hopped off to one of his favorite berry patches and picked some treats
for her to try.

He hopped back and put some berries next to the hedgehog and waited.

But she was silent and still.

Thumper was stumped.

"Don't they smell good?" Thumper asked her. "I'm sure they taste good.
They're from my favorite berry patch."

Thumper sniffed them and decided to make sure they were as good as he remembered. "Yup. They *are* delicious!" Thumper told her. "At least I think so." He giggled.

But the hedgehog still hadn't said anything.

Thumper didn't know what to do. He hopped over to his father.

"Papa," he said, "why won't the hedgehog be my friend? I've been really nice. I tickled her with a feather, and I brought her berry treats. I even invited her to play tag, and she didn't want to play with me."

Papa Bunny smiled. "Not everyone makes friends right away. Give her a little time," he suggested.

Thumper nodded and hopped over to his sisters.

He decided to keep playing in the forest with his sisters, and maybe the hedgehog would come out and play on her own when she was ready.

So he and his sisters continued to scamper and chase each other through the meadow. They darted and they raced. . . .

But still no hedgehog.

Then the bunnies jumped and joked with their butterfly friends. They hoppcd and leaped and laughed as they played in the flower fields.

But still no sign of a hedgehog. . . .

Thumper looked around, but he didn't see her.

Little did he know, the little hedgehog was watching from behind a bush as Thumper and his sisters played. She was *almost* ready to join in on their fun.

Lots of time had gone by, and Thumper decided to return to the tree he had found the hedgehog sleeping by earlier in the day.

"Want to be friends?" he called to the hedgehog.

But there was no answer.

He crept behind the tree to the sleeping nook and discovered the hedgehog was gone!

"Where are you?" Thumper said. "I wanted to be friends."

Then Thumper heard a small voice coming from behind him.

"Hello," someone said. "May I play tag with you and your sisters?"

It was the little hedgehog!

"Of course you can play with us," Thumper said.

"And maybe we can be friends?" the hedgehog asked.

Thumper smiled. "I'd love to be your friend," he said.

So that afternoon, under the warm, bright summer sun, five little bunnies and one little hedgehog played tag in the forest.

The hedgehog chased while Daisy wriggled and Trixie slid, Ria giggled and Tessie hid, and Thumper smiled . . . because they had made a new friend.